Haley's Wish

Navina Magesh Kumar

AuthorHouse™
1663 Liberty Drive
Bloomington, IN 47403
www.authorhouse.com
Phone: 1-800-839-8640

First published by AuthorHouse   04/30/11

ISBN: 978-1-4567-6318-3 (sc)

Library of Congress Control Number: 2011906819

Printed in the United States of America

This book is printed on acid-free paper.

authorHOUSE®

To all my friends & family, especially Maya Auntie.

Haley wistfully stared at many people walking their pet dogs down the street. They were cute, cuddly, and furry dogs. "I wish I had a pup to play with and cuddle with," Haley murmured in her mind. Then, she quickly scurried into her classroom like a little mouse. Just like a little mouse.

"Hi!" yelled Emma cheerfully with a huge grin on her face. She looked like she'd just won a million dollars! Before Haley could even open her mouth Emma blabbered out "I got a puppy yesterday!"

"That's great" replied Haley without any enthusiasm in her voice.

After school was over, Haley ran the entire way to her house. When her mom opened the door, Haley took a deep breath then desperately blurted out "Can I get a puppy?" Haley's mother sighed heavily.

"Haley honey, haven't we been through this before?" she asked in a gentle and soft but a little annoyed tone. "We can't afford a pet and it's too much work" her mother explained for the tenth time.

"FINE!" yelled Haley with her face a bright scarlet. Next, she stormed up the wooden stairs with a loud thud every step she took. "Thud, thud, thud" her feet chanted. Her mom sighed and went back to work.

5

Once she was in her room, she flopped onto her bed thinking hard about what to do to change her mom and dad's mind. She knew that her dad wouldn't let her get a pet either because she had asked him the day before. Of course, his reply had been a blunt no. That was the response she had expected and Haley had to admit that they couldn't afford a pet. On the other hand, she did know that she could definitely take good care of one. "Bingo! I can pet sit other dogs and cats!" exclaimed Haley getting a bit brighter.

First, she decided to make big posters that gave information about her new service. Haley jumped off her bed and got to work. She got crayons, markers, colored pencils, and many other art supplies to use. Careful not to mess up, she wrote this on the flier in big bold letters: Need a pet sitter? Well, here's your answer! When that was done she wrote down all the details about her new service in her neatest handwriting. Then, she decided to make copies of her flier to put in people's mailboxes.

"Mom, can I use the copy machine?" Haley called loud enough so her mother could hear her perfectly.

"Sure" answered her mother. So she swiftly made 30 copies of her flier.

"One...two...three" she counted as the papers came out one after another. She decided that she could take more copies after she used up the ones she already had. Haley made sure to leave the original flier in her room so she could take more copies later.

As soon as the last sheet slipped out, Haley snatched it and zoomed down the stairs eagerly almost tripping on the way. Next, she slipped into her favorite sweatshirt. It had a golden star shimmering on it. "I'm going outside for awhile" Haley told her parents.

"Okay" permitted her dad.

After a half hour or so, Haley came back into the house, but this time her hands were empty. An hour later the phone rang. Haley leaped up and grabbed the ringing phone from the table like a tiger would when it was hunting its prey. She hoped and hoped and hoped that it was her first customer. But to her disappointment it was just her friend Leslie who had a doubt about today's spelling homework.

Soon the phone rang again. "Hello" greeted a familiar voice that Haley recognized easily.

"Hello, Mrs. Smith" she replied.

"I saw your ad about the service you are doing," Mrs. Smith said. "And I was wondering if you could pet sit Toby, my pet dog tomorrow at 11:00 a.m." she continued.

"Sure!" exclaimed Haley trying to jot down the details messily in a notebook she found nearby. Then, she hung up and squealed with joy.

After dinner, Haley went to bed and slowly drifted off to a deep slumber thinking about the next day...

Sunlight slid through the window and climbed on top of Haley's face covering it like a warm and cozy blanket. Haley twisted and turned. Finally, she sat up on her bed. She took a quick glance at the alarm clock. The time was exactly 9:54. She brushed her teeth and sprinted downstairs for breakfast.

Haley ate up all of her French toast as fast as she could. She took a nice hot shower and noticed that the time was already 10:30. Immediately, she bundled up with all her clothes and then slipped on her shoes. Haley ran outside heading to Mrs. Smith's house. Since her house was only a few blocks away, it was not a painfully long walk.

"DING DONG" rang the doorbell when Haley pushed the button. "Hi Haley" Mrs. Smith greeted as she led Haley inside. She could see a cute collie sprawled on the cold floor. *That must be Toby.* Haley thought. "My phone number is hanging on the refrigerator" Mrs. Smith informed Haley briefly. "Oh, and I'll call if there happens to be a slight delay in my return," she said. Haley nodded.

Mrs. Smith had just driven away in her car when Toby ran to a table nearby and pushed a beautiful vase over. Haley dashed toward it and caught it a second before it would have crashed into tiny pieces. "Bad dog" she tried to scold Toby even though she knew he couldn't understand a word she was saying. Haley couldn't help but smile at the naughty dog. She decided the best thing to do was take him outdoors.

She carefully led Toby out and threw a twig for him to fetch. Instead of getting it, he splashed right into a mud puddle! Haley groaned. They kept playing for a little while despite the fact that Toby now looked like he had taken a shower with chocolate ice cream.

Next, Haley gave him a bath and brushed him. When she finished, Mrs. Smith came back. "How was everything?" she asked Haley.

"Pretty good" responded Haley. Then, Mrs. Smith handed Haley $25. "Thanks" called Haley already heading for the door. On the way out, Haley gave Toby a quick pat and was gone before he knew it.

After she had got home, Haley told her parents all about Toby's mischief. "Wow" they had said in unison, obviously impressed.

During dinner that night, Haley's parents told her they wanted to talk to her. "Well..." her mom started as her voice trailed off.

"We think you can get a puppy" finished her father. "But you have to earn your own money for pet food and accessories" he added with a slight smile. There was a small twinkle in both of their eyes. Haley could thoroughly see that they were both enjoying this.

21

"You can use the $25 I earned" offered Haley getting more excited every moment.

"That might just do for now," her mom hesitantly conceded. It was obvious that she wasn't fully convinced yet.

"Yes, I suppose it should" agreed Haley's father.

"Oh, thank you so much!!!" shrieked Haley while she hugged her parents tightly.

CPSIA information can be obtained
at www.ICGtesting.com
233193LV00001B